A WHITE HERON

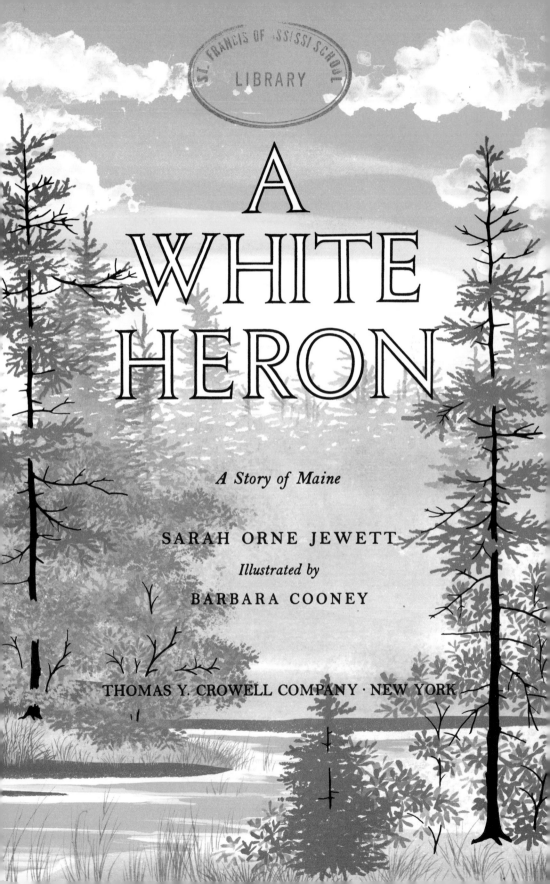

A WHITE HERON

A Story of Maine

SARAH ORNE JEWETT

Illustrated by

BARBARA COONEY

THOMAS Y. CROWELL COMPANY · NEW YORK

I

The woods were already filled with shadows one June evening, though a bright sunset still glimmered faintly among the trunks of the trees. With a twig of birch leaves a girl was driving home her cow, a plodding, provoking creature, but a valued companion for all that. They were going away from whatever light there was and striking deep into the woods, but their feet were familiar with the path and it was no matter whether their eyes could see it or not.

1

There was hardly a night the summer through when the old cow could be found waiting at the pasture bars; on the contrary, it was her greatest pleasure to hide herself away among the huckleberry bushes, and though she wore a loud bell she had made the discovery that if she stood perfectly still it would not ring. So Sylvia had to hunt for her until she found her, calling "Co'! Co'!" with never an

2

answering moo, until her patience was quite spent. But sometimes in pleasant weather the cow's pranks became a game of hide and seek, and as the child had no playmates she lent herself to this amusement with zest.

Once found, however, the old cow was not inclined to wander farther. She even turned in the right direction as they left the pasture and stepped along the road at a good pace.

3

She was quite ready to be milked now and seldom stopped to browse.

Sylvia wondered what her grandmother would say because they were so late. It was a great while since she had left home at half-past five o'clock on this June evening, but everybody knew the difficulty of making the errand a short one. Mrs. Tilley had chased the horned torment too many summer evenings herself to blame anyone else for lingering, and as she waited she was only thankful that nowadays she had Sylvia to give such valuable assistance. The good woman suspected that her granddaughter loitered occasionally on her own account; there never was such a child for straying about out-of-doors since the world was made!

The companions followed the shady wood-road, the cow taking slow steps and the child very fast ones. The cow stopped long at the brook to drink, as if the pasture were not half a swamp, and Sylvia stood still and waited, letting her bare feet cool themselves in the shoal water while the great twilight moths struck softly against her. She waded on through the brook as the cow moved away, and listened to the thrushes with a heart that beat fast with pleasure.

There was a stirring in the great boughs overhead. They were full of little birds and beasts that seemed to be wide awake and going about their world or else saying good night to each other in sleepy twitters. Sylvia herself felt sleepy as she walked along. However, it was not much farther to the house and the air was soft and sweet.

She was not often in the woods so late as this, and it made her feel as if she were a part of the gray shadows and the moving leaves. She was thinking how long it seemed since she first came to her grandmother's farm a year ago, and wondering if everything went on in the noisy town just the same as when she was there.

Suddenly she was horror-stricken to hear a clear whistle not very far away. Not a bird's whistle, which would have a sort of friendliness, but a boy's whistle, determined and somewhat aggressive. Sylvia left the cow to whatever sad fate might await her and stepped discreetly aside into the underbrush, but she was just too late. The enemy had discovered her, and he called out in a cheerful and persuasive tone, "Halloa, little girl, how far is it to the road?"

Trembling, Sylvia answered almost inaudibly, "A good ways."

She did not dare to look boldly at the tall young man, who carried a gun over his shoulder, but she came out of the bushes and again followed the cow, while he walked alongside.

"I have been hunting for some birds," the stranger said kindly, "and I have lost my way and need a friend very much. Don't be afraid," he added gallantly. "Speak up and tell me what your name is and whether you think I can spend the night at your house and go out gunning early in the morning."

Sylvia was more alarmed than before. Would not her grandmother consider her much to blame for this? She hung her head as

if the stem of it were broken, but she managed
to answer "Sylvy" with much effort when her
companion again asked her name.

Mrs. Tilley was standing in the doorway
when the trio came into view. The cow gave a
loud moo by way of explanation.

"Yes, you'd better speak up for yourself,
you old trial! Where'd she hide herself away
this time, Sylvy?" But Sylvia kept an awed
silence; she knew by instinct that her grandmother did not comprehend the gravity of the
situation. She must be mistaking the stranger
for one of the farmer-lads of the region.

The young man stood his gun beside the
door and dropped a lumpy gamebag beside it;
then he bade Mrs. Tilley good evening and
after repeating his wayfarer's story, asked if
he could have a night's lodging.

"Put me anywhere you like," he said. "I
must be off early in the morning, before day;
but I am very hungry indeed. You can give me
some milk at any rate, that's plain."

"Dear sakes, yes," responded the hostess,
whose long-slumbering hospitality seemed

10

now to be awakened. "You might fare better
if you went out to the main road a mile or so,
but you're welcome to what we've got. I'll
milk right off, and you make yourself at home.
You can sleep on husks or feathers," she
proffered graciously. "I raised them all myself. There's good pasturing for geese just below here. Now step round and set a plate for
the gentleman, Sylvy!" And Sylvia promptly
stepped. She was glad to have something to
do, and she was hungry herself.

11

The young man was delighted to find so clean and comfortable a little dwelling in this New England wilderness. He listened eagerly to the old woman's quaint talk, watched Sylvia's pale face and shining gray eyes with ever growing enthusiasm, and insisted that this was the best supper he had eaten for a month. Afterward the new-made friends sat down in the doorway together watching the moon come up.

Soon it would be berry time, and Sylvia was a great help at picking. The cow was a good milker, though a plaguey thing to keep track of, the hostess gossiped frankly, adding presently that she had buried four children, including Sylvia's mother, so that a son (who might be dead) in California was all the family she had left. "Dan, my boy, was a great hand to go gunning," she explained sadly. "I never wanted for pa'tridges or gray squer'ls while he was to home. He's been a great wand'rer, I expect, and he's no hand to write letters. There, I don't blame him, I'd ha' seen the world myself if it had been so I could.

"Sylvy takes after him," the grandmother continued affectionately, after a minute's pause. "There ain't a foot o' ground she don't know her way over, and the wild creatures counts her one o' themselves. Squer'ls she'll tame to come an' feed right out o' her hands, and all sorts o' birds. Last winter she got the jay-birds to feeding here, and I believe she'd a' scanted herself of her own meals to have plenty to throw out amongst 'em, if I hadn't kep' watch. Anything but crows, I tell her, I'm willin' to help support—though Dan he had a tamed one o' them that did seem to have

14

reason same as folks. It was 'round here a good spell after he went away."

"So Sylvy knows all about birds, does she?" the boy exclaimed, as he looked round at the little girl who sat, very demure but increasingly sleepy, in the moonlight. "I am making a collection of birds myself. I have been at it ever since I was young."

Mrs. Tilley smiled.

"There are two or three very rare ones I have been hunting for these five years," he continued. "I mean to get them on my own ground if they can be found."

"Do you cage 'em up?" asked Mrs. Tilley doubtfully, in response to this enthusiastic announcement.

"Oh no, they're stuffed and preserved, dozens and dozens of them," said the ornithologist, "and I have shot or snared every one myself. I caught a glimpse of a heron a few miles from here on Saturday, and I have followed it in this direction. They have never been found in this district at all. A *white* heron, it is."

He turned again to look at Sylvia with the hope of discovering that the rare bird was one of her acquaintances.

15

But Sylvia was watching a hop toad in the narrow footpath.

"You would know the heron if you saw it," the stranger continued eagerly. "A queer tall white bird with soft feathers and long thin legs. And it would have a nest perhaps in the top of a high tree, made of sticks, something like a hawk's nest."

Sylvia's heart gave a wild beat; she knew that strange white bird and had once stolen softly near where it stood in some bright green swamp grass, over at the other side of the woods. There was an open place where the sunshine always seemed strangely yellow and hot, where tall, nodding rushes grew. Her

17

grandmother had warned her that she might sink in the soft black mud underneath and never be heard of more. Not far beyond were the salt marshes just this side of the sea itself, which Sylvia wondered and dreamed much about but never had seen. Its great voice could sometimes be heard above the noise of the woods on stormy nights.

"I can't think of anything I should like so much as to find that heron's nest," the handsome stranger was saying. "I would give ten dollars to anybody who could show it to me," he added desperately, "and I mean to spend my whole vacation hunting for it if need be. Perhaps it was only migrating, or had been chased out of its own region by some bird of prey."

Mrs. Tilley gave amazed attention to all this, but Sylvia still watched the toad, not divining, as she might have done at some calmer time, that the creature wished to get to its hole under the doorstep and was much hindered by the unusual spectators at that hour of the evening.

No amount of thought that night could decide how many wished-for treasures the ten dollars, so lightly spoken of, would buy.

The next day the young sportsman hovered about the woods, and Sylvia kept him company, having lost her first fear of the friendly lad, who proved to be most kind and sympathetic. He told her many things about the birds and what they knew and where they lived and what they did with themselves. And he gave her a jackknife, which she thought as great a treasure as if she were a desert islander.

All day long he did not once make her troubled or afraid except when he brought down some unsuspecting singing creature from its bough. Sylvia would have liked him vastly better without his gun; she could not understand why he killed the very birds he seemed to like so much. But as the day waned, Sylvia still watched the young man with loving admiration. She had never seen anybody so charming and delightful.

They stopped to listen to a bird's song; they pressed forward again eagerly, parting the branches, speaking to each other rarely and in whispers; the young man going first and Sylvia following, fascinated, a few steps behind.

She grieved because the longed-for white heron was elusive, but she did not lead the guest, she only followed, and there was no such thing as speaking first. The sound of her own unquestioned voice would have terrified her—it was hard enough to answer yes or no when there was need of that. At last evening began to fall and they drove the cow home together. Sylvia smiled with pleasure when they came to the place where she had heard his whistle only the night before.

II

Half a mile from home, at the farther edge of the woods, a great pine tree stood, the last of its generation. Whether it was left for a boundary mark, or for what reason, no one could say; the woodchoppers who had felled its mates were dead and gone long ago, and a whole forest of sturdy trees—pines and oaks and maples—had grown again. But the stately head of this old pine towered above them all and made a landmark for sea and shore miles and miles away.

Sylvia knew it well. She had always believed that whoever climbed to the top of it

could see the ocean; and she had often laid her hand on the great rough trunk and looked up wistfully at those dark boughs that the wind always stirred, no matter how hot and still the air might be below.

Now she thought of the tree with a new excitement, for why, if one climbed it at break of day, could not one see all the world and easily discover from whence the white heron flew, and mark the place and find the hidden nest?

All night the door of the little house stood open, and the whippoorwills came and sang upon the very step. The young sportsman and his old hostess were sound asleep, but Sylvia's great design kept her awake and watching.

The short summer night seemed as long as the winter darkness. At last, when the whippoorwills ceased and she was afraid the morning would, after all, come too soon, she stole out of the house. She followed the pasture path through the woods, hastening toward the open ground beyond. She listened with a sense of comfort and companionship to the drowsy twitter of a half-awakened bird, whose perch she had jarred in passing.

There was the huge tree asleep in the paling moonlight, and small Sylvia began bravely to mount to the top of it. Her bare feet and fingers pinched and held like bird's claws to the monstrous ladder reaching up, up, almost to the sky itself.

First she must mount the white oak tree that grew alongside; there she was almost lost among the dark branches and the green leaves heavy and wet with dew; a bird fluttered off its nest, and a red squirrel ran to and fro pettishly scolding. Sylvia felt her way with ease. She had often climbed there and she knew that higher still one of the oak's upper branches chafed against the pine trunk, just where its lower boughs were set close together. Only when she made the dangerous pass from one tree to the other would the great enterprise really begin.

She crept out along the swaying oak limb at last and took the daring step across into the old pine tree. The way was harder than she thought; she must reach far and hold fast. The sharp dry twigs caught and held her and scratched her like angry talons, the pitch made her thin little fingers clumsy and stiff as she went round and round the tree's great stem, higher and higher upward. The tree seemed to lengthen itself out as she went. The sparrows and robins in the woods below were beginning to wake and twitter to the dawn, yet it seemed much lighter there aloft in the pine tree. She knew she must hurry.

When finally the last thorny bough was past, and Sylvia stood, trembling and tired but wholly triumphant, high in the treetop. There was the sea with the dawning sun making a golden dazzle over it, and toward that glorious east flew two hawks with slow-moving pinions. How low they looked in the air from that height when one had seen them before only far up and dark against the blue sky. Their gray feathers were as soft as moths; they seemed only a little way from the tree, and Sylvia felt as if she too could go flying away among the clouds. Westward, the woodlands and farms reached miles and miles into the distance; here and there were church steeples and white villages.

The birds sang louder and louder. At last the sun came up bewilderingly bright. The clouds that had been purple and rose-colored and yellow began to fade away. Sylvia could see the white sails of ships out at sea.

Where was the white heron's nest in the green branches? Was this wonderful sight and pageant of the world the only reward for having climbed to such a giddy height? Now look down again, Sylvia, where the green marsh is set among the shining birches and

dark hemlocks; there, where you saw the white heron once, you will see him again; look, look! A white spot of him like a single floating feather comes up from the dead hemlock and grows larger, and rises, and comes close at last, and goes by the landmark pine with steady sweep of wing and outstretched slender neck and crested head. And wait! wait! Do not move a foot or a finger, for the heron has perched on a pine bough not far beyond yours, and cries back to his mate on the nest and plumes his feathers for the new day!

Sylvia gave a long sigh a minute later when a company of shouting catbirds came to the tree; vexed by their fluttering and lawlessness the solemn heron flew away. Sylvia knew his secret now—the wild, light, slender bird that floated and wavered and went back like an arrow to his home in the green world beneath.

Well satisfied, she made her perilous way down again, not daring to look far below the branch she stood on, ready to cry sometimes because her fingers ached and her feet slipped. She wondered over and over again what the stranger would say to her, and what he would think when she told him how to find his way straight to the heron's nest.

"Sylvy, Sylvy!" called the grandmother again and again, but nobody answered. The small husk bed was empty and Sylvia had disappeared.

The guest waked from a dream and remembering his day's pleasure hurried to dress himself. He was sure from the way the shy little girl looked once or twice yesterday that she had seen the white heron, and now she must really be made to tell. Here she was coming now, paler than ever, and her worn old frock was torn and tattered and smeared with pine pitch. The splendid moment had come to speak of the dead hemlock tree by the green marsh.

But Sylvia did not speak after all, though the old grandmother fretfully rebuked her, and the young man's kind, appealing eyes were looking straight in her own.

What is it that suddenly forbids her and makes her dumb? Has she been nine years growing and now, when the great world for the first time puts out a hand to her, must she thrust it aside for a bird's sake? The murmur of the pine's green branches is in her ears; she remembers how the white heron came flying through the golden air and how they watched the sea and the morning together, and Sylvia

cannot speak; she cannot tell the heron's secret and give its life away.

Sylvia suffered a sharp pang as the guest
went away disappointed later in the day. Many
a night she heard the echo of his whistle haunt-
ing the pasture path as she came home with
the loitering cow. Were the birds better
friends than their hunter might have been?
Who can tell?

ABOUT THE ILLUSTRATOR

In describing her feelings about the illustration of *A White Heron*, Barbara Cooney said that the coast of Maine is the place she loves best in the world. "I wanted to make pictures showing what I love about it, the mists rising among the trees, the superimposed layers of countryside and trees separated by rising mists or incoming fogs, the feeling of the place—something like an ethereal Japanese screen."

In 1958 Miss Cooney received the Caldecott Medal for *Chanticleer and the Fox*. She was born in Brooklyn, New York, grew up on Long Island and in Maine, and currently lives in a small Massachusetts town with her husband, a physician, and her four children. Miss Cooney received her B.A. degree from Smith College and served as a WAC during World War II.

ABOUT THE AUTHOR

Sarah Orne Jewett drew upon her own rural Maine background for the settings and subjects of her stories. She was born in South Berwick, Maine, in 1849, and spent much of her girlhood there, accompanying her father, a doctor, as he made his rounds. Her best-known works include the short stories *A White Heron*, *The King of Folly Island*, and *A Native of Winby*, which appear in a book of loosely connected sketches about a Maine community, entitled *The Country of the Pointed Firs and Other Stories*. Miss Jewett died in 1909.